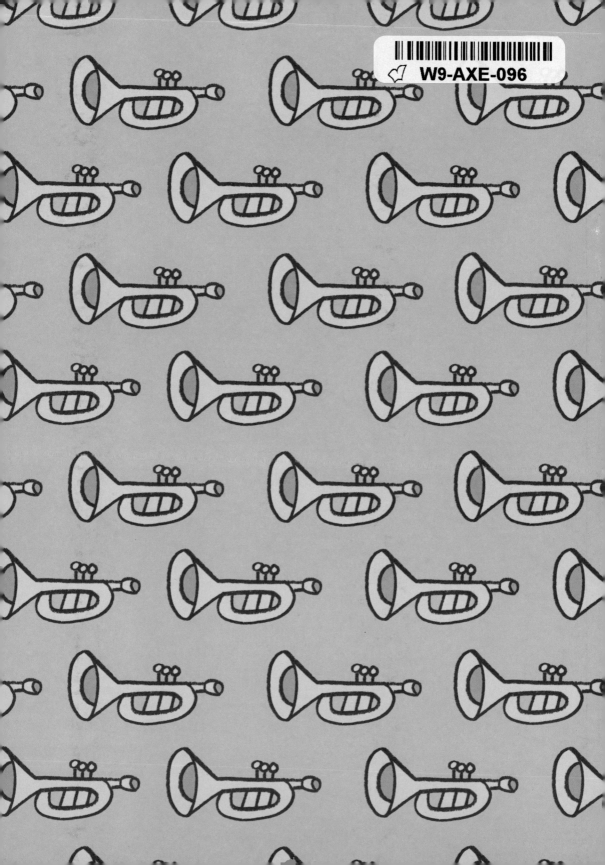

To Mr. Trimmer
*Blaaarp!*

Printed in Singapore
Reinforced binding

First Edition
10 9 8 7 6 5 4 3 2 1
F850-6835-5-11288

Library of Congress Cataloging-in-Publication Data

Willems, Mo.
 Listen to my trumpet! / by Mo Willems.
    p.  cm.
 Summary: When Piggie plays her new trumpet for Gerald, the elephant decides he must be
honest in his response.
 ISBN 978-1-4231-5404-4 (storybook/picturebook)
[1. Pigs—Fiction. 2. Elephants—Fiction. 3. Trumpet—Fiction. 4. Friendship—Fiction.]  I. Title.
 PZ7.W65535Li 2012
 [E]—dc23                      2011012095

Visit www.hyperionbooksforchildren.com and www.pigeonpresents.com

By Mo Willems

# Listen to My Trumpet!

An ELEPHANT & PIGGIE Book

Hyperion Books for Children / *New York*

AN IMPRINT OF DISNEY BOOK GROUP

Gerald!

5

Wait.

That was
not right.

17

21

22

And now the
BIG FINISH!

28

Finished!

So?!

What do you think
of my trumpet?

And . . . ?

You, uh, hold your trumpet very well.

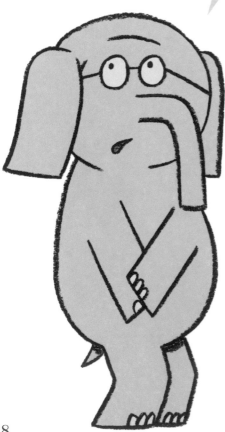

I'm waiting. . . .

Piggie. You
are my friend.

And I am
your friend.

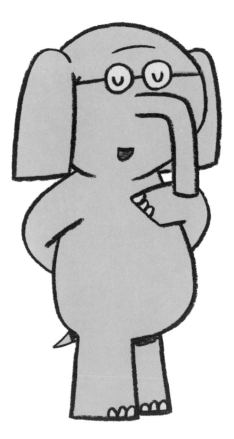

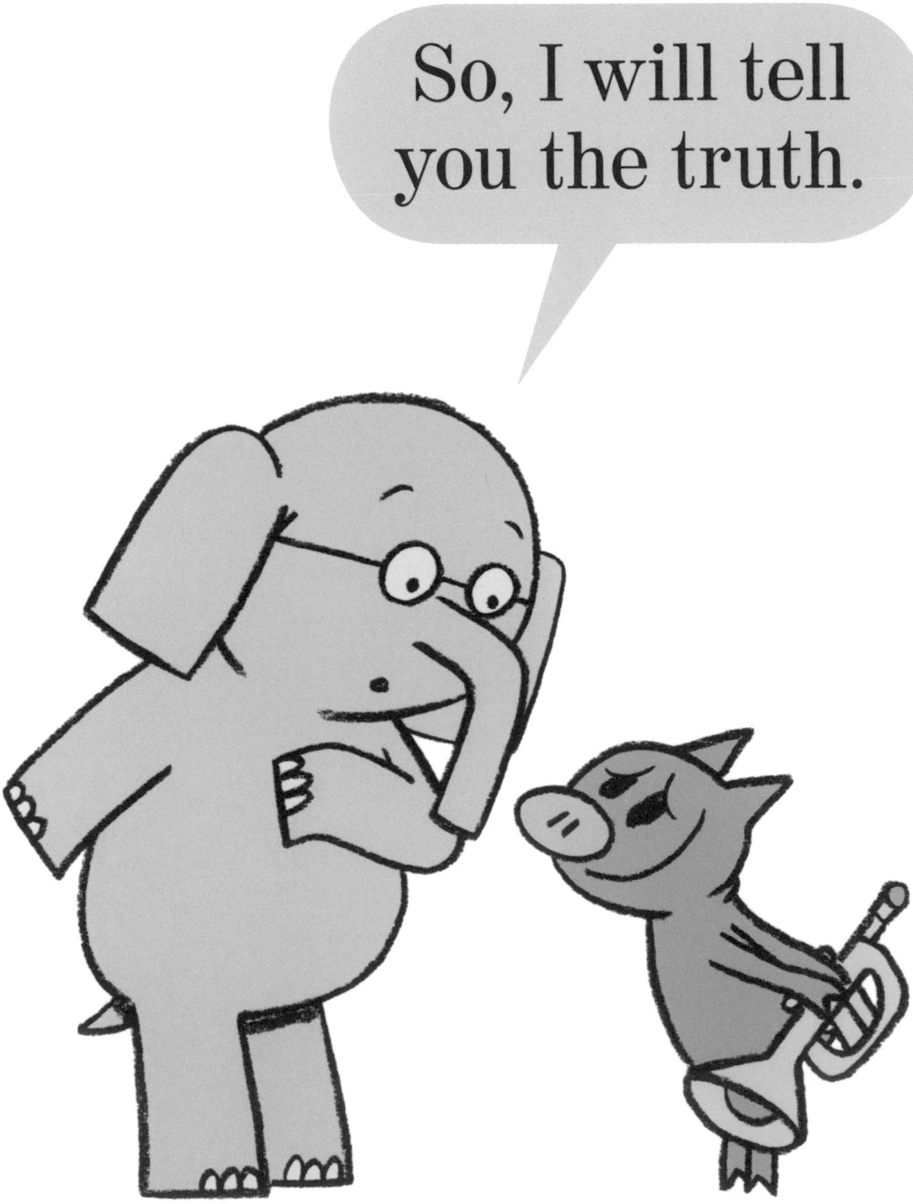
So, I will tell you the truth.

I want to sound
like you.

# Elephant and Piggie have more funny adventures in:

Today I Will Fly!

My Friend Is Sad

I Am Invited to a Party!

There Is a Bird on Your Head!

I Love My New Toy!

I Will Surprise My Friend!

Are You Ready to Play Outside?

Watch Me Throw the Ball!

Elephants Cannot Dance!

Pigs Make Me Sneeze!

I Am Going!

Can I Play Too?

We Are in a Book!

I Broke My Trunk!

Should I Share My Ice Cream?

Happy Pig Day!